Amazing ANIMAL EARTH

Alessandra Yap and Anastasia Popp

Little Steps
PUBLISHING

There are so many animals
living near and far,
it's almost impossible to know
just how many there are!

At your house you might have
a dog, a cat, or a mouse,
but if we explore, we will certainly find
animals you can't find in your house!

First we'll stop in
AFRICA,
whose many
countries contain
animals of all kinds...
like the lion with his
bushy mane!

There's an aardvark shuffling along slow,
an impala and gazelle bounding away,
a chimpanzee with a stolen bow,
and a hippopotamus who just wants to lay.

A giraffe who towers so tall,
and a rhinoceros so very fat,
an elephant with a trumpeting call,
and lemurs the size of a rat.

There's a wildebeest with a hairy nose,
warthogs with angry tusks,
elands that run like pros,
and zebras that gallop across husks.

In *Europe* there are deer that prance,
wolverines and wolves that stalk,
elegant weasels that dance,
and a nattering fox that wants to talk.

There's a tall brown bear, lounging to rest,
moose with giant antlers on their heads,
lynx and badgers that wander the forest,
and reindeer that pull Santa's sled,

Asia's animals will have you in awe;
water buffalo who are happy to graze
tigers with sharp teeth and claws,
and tapirs and langurs nap in a daze.

The red panda is a rare sight,
Asian elephants bring good luck.
Sometimes the gibbons will have a play fight,
causing the orangutans to shriek and duck.

While in **NORTH AMERICA** you might spy
a solid brown bison on the plain,
a majestic eagle in the sky,
or mustangs trying to steal some grain.

There are raccoons with masked faces,
bears both grizzly and black,
otters with muddy hiding places
and alligators waiting for a snack.

You might spot a beaver or groundhog,
or even the soft-coated mink.
A mountain lion going out for a jog,
or a skunk with a terrible stink!

In SOUTH AMERICA
a kinkajou hides in the trees,
the cougar and jaguar stalk prey,
the tapeti and tamandua do as they please,
the armadillo and sloth relax and play.

AUSTRALIA is our furthest trip yet,
where kangaroos and wallabies jump.
There, bilbies and possums sneak out at sunset,
and wombats hide in a clump.

You might discover a potoroo,
or koalas who climb eucalypt trees,
echidnas and platypus star at the zoo,
and the sugar gliders soar with ease.

In ANTARCTICA, way down south,
there are many kinds of seals;
fur, elephant and leopard, who laugh with mirth,
    and try to avoid being the orca's meals.

        Two types of penguins – Adelie and Emperor,
            march across the ice and snow ...

You have been quite an adventurer -
look how many animals you now know!